Stellarella It's Saturday!

Story by Deborah W. Dykes

Illustrations by Christina Mattison Ebert-Klaven

"There is nothing more powerful than an Idea whose time has come."
—Victor Hugo (b.1802 d.1885)

This book is dedicated to **Stella Elizabeth Shdeed**, my granddaughter, whom I hope to see again soon. I live and play with her through my writing of "Stellarella" books.

To my granddaughters, Poet Mahoney Harris and Violette Eden Harris, two bundles of love and laughter and who bring out the wild and crazy "Yaya" in me. To my granddaughters, Elizabeth Grace Tweit, Isabelle Kelley, and Lyla June Kelley who invite me into an imaginary world of adventure and excitement. To little Sydney Livingston Shafer, who brings a smile to my face each time I hear her say, "Silly Yaya!"

This book is written to little girls all over the world. Be creative, be encouraged and know that you are created in the image of God.

From Christina, to Marshal, whose contagious energy, unrelenting passion and indomitable spirit bring dreams into reality - may your love and light continue to guide our life together.

Illustrations by Christina Ebert-Klaven

Produced by Maine Authors Publishing
www.maineauthorspublishing.com

Printed in the United States of America

Library of Congress Cataloging-in-Publication Data
Registration Number: TXu 1-814-158

Stellarella, LLC, December 11, 2012

Dykes, Deborah W.
Stellarella! It's Saturday!
SUMMARY: Introduces young children to a cast of female characters who offer a variety of role models who can inspire and encourage.

PREFACE

Stellarella, a feisty, frizzy-headed five-year-old, has an indomitable spirit, sassy style and creative imagination that make her irresistible to any young reader. In *Stellarella: It's Saturday*!, Stellarella and her herculean and intuitive bulldog, named "Tank," go on an imaginary trip to the local farmer's market where they meet a diverse cast of vibrant and independent female characters: Ms. Maria with her zucchini fritters, Ms. Leanna with her tomato toast, and Ms. Thibodeaux with her bodacious banjo! Sadly, the actual market trip is rained out. But the rain does not dampen Stellarella's exuberant spirit. By the end of the day, Stellarella learns that disappointment can be turned into something surprisingly happy and fun.

In *Stellarella! It's Saturday!* Stellarella and Tank experience a world in which women are independent, educated, self-sufficient, healthy, and powerful. They encounter adult women who are culturally and ethnically diverse, and who are very willing to share their talents and gifts with inquisitive and curious children. *Stellarella! It's Saturday!* introduces young children to a cast of female characters who offer a variety of role models who can inspire and encourage.

Like so many things that grow out of personal struggle, my writing of *Stellarella* grew out of my experience of growing up as a girl, being a woman, and then as ordained clergy in the Episcopal church, in a culture constructed to support male dominance. Why wound our little girls with language that takes place under a male-dominant faith? Why not expose our children to a gender inclusive God? Why should a little girl have to experience being less human, less significant, than a little boy simply because "she" is not created in the image of God?

One of the most astounding contributions to *Stellarella* has been made by the artist-illustrator, Christina Mattison Ebert-Klaven. Christina read *Stellarella* and then responded with marvelous, perfect illustrations drawn out of her own insights and spirit.

During the early stages of writing *Stellarella*, my husband, David, and my closest friends, Anne K. Perry and Alan W. Perry, rallied my spirit, championed my cause, and stirred my creative impulses. So, thank you to my dear friends Anne and Alan Perry, and to my friends Anky and Mary Ann Petro who offered support, and encouragement. To Amy Perry, Julie Perry, and Lucy Perry, who filled a void in my heart. My dear friends John Dominic Crossan and Sarah Crossan asked the important questions that gave depth and richness to my text. My close friends, Joan Chittister, OSB, and Maureen Tobin, OSB, two beautifully unique and sacred women offered their gifts of kindness and encouragement to this work. To Helen Rieger who early on helped me experiment with the Stellarella character.

I owe much to my daughters, Jennifer Tweit and Suzanna Kelley, who bring me comfort and buoy my spirit. To Clint and Amy Harris, my son and daughter-in-law who have remained present, supportive and loving. To Julie Harris Shdeed, because hope abides.

Finally, to David, my husband, my partner, my love, my champion, who in very special ways makes my life exquisite. It is David who gives depth and meaning to all that I do and all that I am.

It's Saturday! **Tank! Wake Up!**

It's Saturday and we are going to the market!
A trip to the market is always an adventure!
You can wear your bulldog collar with the sparkles, Tank.
I will wear my glittery headband with the colorful feathers.

While Mama and I make breakfast and plan our trip to the market, Tank, would you please help watch my little sister, Sydney? Instead of eating her oats, she will probably play with her cereal and feed most of it to you, Tank.

I love going to the market!

It has so many things to see and so many good things to eat.

Ms. O'Reilly has a cantaloupe stand and sells fresh cantaloupe.

Cantaloupe is delicious and good for us, too.

It's your favorite, Tank!

Mama said that the tomatoes are especially ripe and yummy this time of year, just right for **tomato toast.**

When we get there, I will say to Ms. Leanna,

'May I have **two** bright red tomatoes, **please?'**

Ms. Leanna grows tomatoes all year long in a warm greenhouse.

Let's get some yellow squash
and zucchini, Tank.

Later, when we come home,
we will help Mama make zucchini fritters.

You know how much we love
fried zucchini fritters.

Tank, did you know *zucchini* is Italian?

Grazie!
    Arrivederci!
      Ciao!

Ms. Maria always speaks to me in Italian.

She says, '*Buon giorno, Stellarella! Come stai oggi?*'

I will say to Ms. Maria,
'*Ciao, Ms. Maria. Io sono buono oggi!*'

This means, 'Hello, Ms. Maria. I am well!'

Then, I will say to Ms. Maria,
'May I have three yellow squash
and four zucchini, *per favore!* Please!'

Ms. Sadie makes the best jelly and plum preserves I have **ever** tasted.

We'll buy a big jar of her **strawberry jelly.**

"Mama, will you please add two jars of Ms. Sadie's strawberry jelly to your shopping list? Tank and I love strawberry jelly on **biscuits!**"

Tank, did you know God makes **strawberries**?

She grows them from seeds she plants in the dirt.

Did you know she makes squash and zucchini, carrots and corn?

God makes rainbows and rabbits, bubbles and brown bears— **she's as busy as Mama!**

God makes **everything** we see at the market.

Tank, do you know what my favorite thing is to see and do at the market?

My favorite thing of all is **Ms. Thibodeaux** and her **bodacious banjo**.

Ms. Thibodeaux can play the banjo better than **anyone** in the **whole world**.

If she's wearing her tropical pink muumuu, I will compliment Ms. Thibodeaux and say, 'You're looking very pretty today, Ms. Thibodeaux.'

Ms. Thibodeaux can strum and bounce, twirl and toss, sing and laugh with such joy she makes everyone happy, especially me!

Tank, even you prance and dance when Ms. Thibodeaux plays her banjo.

"Mama, is it almost time to go? Tank and I are **ready**!"

Come on, Tank. Let's wait outside for Mama and Sydney.

Oh no!
It's raining!

The streets are filled with water!

It's raining really hard. I don't think we can go to the market with all of this rain.

The market will be closed. I am so sad, Tank.

Now my Saturday is *ruined.*

Ruined, ruined, ruined, Tank!

There is nothing to do but stare out of the window and watch it rain.

Humph!

"My goodness, Stellarella!

Why are you and Tank just sitting there? Why are you so sad?" says Mama as she skips into the room.

"Rainy summer days are perfect for Saturday fun!

I'm ready, Stellarella! And so is Sydney.

Are you and Tank ready to play in the rain?"

Tank! Look!
I can't believe my eyes!

Mama is wearing her lime-green and yellow striped swimsuit and her bright blue and pink rain boots with butterflies and bows, and a yellow and red polka-dot rain hat.

And Sydney is wearing her orange swirl swimsuit with a blue dolphin.

Oh my goodness, Tank!
Mama is holding three towels, turquoise swim goggles, a lavender and green umbrella with crickets and stars painted on the fabric, a mesh sack filled with water markers, colorful plastic cups of different sizes, an orange scoop, a pair of bright red flippers, and a plastic purple beach bucket with a green sponge frog and three blue popsicles!

Tank, wait here with Mama and Sydney while I run to my room and change into my black and white polka-dot swimsuit with hot pink trim and a ruffled skirt.

Whoops! I'd better grab my palm tree flip flops!

Hooray!
Let's go play in the rain, Tank!

Did you know God makes rain too, Tank?
She's very clever.

DEBORAH W. DYKES, known to friends and family as "Debo," was born in Shreveport, Louisiana and spent most of her life in the Deep South. She is inspired by the fecund smells of a ripe swamp, eating fried crawfish, oysters-on-the-half-shell, and playing in the rain. Since childhood she has loved walking on stilts, hopping on a pogo stick, and rescuing worms after a heavy summer rain. She is a children's book author of five *Stellarella and Tank* stories and a member of the Society of Children's Book Writers and Illustrators (SCBWI). Before writing children's books, she was an elementary school teacher, middle school science teacher, ordained Episcopal Clergy, and a National Teacher-in-Space finalist. She shares her life with her husband, family, and friends. Readers can follow *Stellarella and Tank* at **www.stellarellaandtank.com**, as well as on Facebook and Twitter.

Originally from Columbia, Maryland, Christina Mattison Ebert-Klaven currently resides in Jackson, Mississippi. She spends most of her time busily attempting to acclimate to the Deep South by practicing her Southern drawl, concealing any paraphernalia that hint at her family's Yankee roots, frying all of her food and subsequently putting out large grease fires. In addition to searching for her inner "Southern-ness," Christina is the artist behind C. Mattison Illustration (www.cmattison.com). She works on a variety of projects including children's books, illustrated maps, book covers and Judaica (Jewish art). She is married to Rabbi Marshal Klaven and they share their home with a toy poodle and a lovebird, whose food Christina occasionally attempts to fry.

This charming little book fills in the spaces in a culture where children and grandmothers get separated as families change and shift and meld and move. It touches the emotional chasm where memories are the only thing left to make the connections real. This book remembers the good things that happened in the past and brings comfort to the empty places in the heart of both child and grandmother. Even better, it promises an even more loving future together. This book is a certain read and a living promise for many.

—JOAN CHITTISTER, OSB, author of *Following the Path*

Dear Mothers & Fathers: This is a beautifully subtle and profoundly intuitive vision in which a young girl's earliest imagination moves instinctively from a mother who runs the kitchen to a God who runs the world. If women produce food and women prepare food, how is God not female? How could it be otherwise, Tank?

—JOHN DOMINIC CROSSAN, author of *The Power of Parable*

$15.95 USD

ISBN-13: 978-1-938883-29-3

51595

9 781938 883293